TONKA MEZZOKA
MEZZANATOR

Status: Weapon of mass destruction
Species: Made by Mezzoka Clan
Galaxy: Milky Way
Traits: Destroys planets, uses super-charged light bullets

www.starfighterbooks.com

Status: Head of the Mezzoka Clan
Species: Mezzoka
Galaxy: Milky Way
Traits: Ruthless leader, compulsive thief

www.starfighterbooks.com

STAR FIGHTERS
EVIL STAR

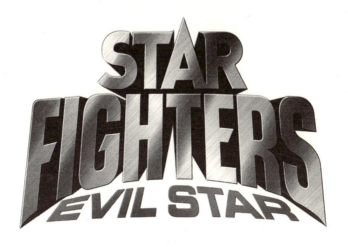

To the Mysterious Dr X

Special thanks to Benjamin Scott

Bloomsbury Publishing, London, New Delhi, New York and Sydney

First published in Great Britain in August 2012 by Bloomsbury Publishing Plc
50 Bedford Square, London, WC1B 3DP

A CIP catalogue record for this book is available from the British Library

ISBN 978 1 4088 2717 8

MIX
Paper from responsible sources
FSC® C018072
FSC www.fsc.org

Typeset by Hewer Text UK Ltd, Edinburgh
Printed in Great Britain by Clays Ltd, St Ives plc, Bungay, Suffolk

1 3 5 7 9 10 8 6 4 2

www.bloomsbury.com
www.starfighterbooks.com

STAR FIGHTERS
EVIL STAR

MAX CHASE

Illustrated by Sam Hadley

BLOOMSBURY

LONDON NEW DELHI NEW YORK SYDNEY

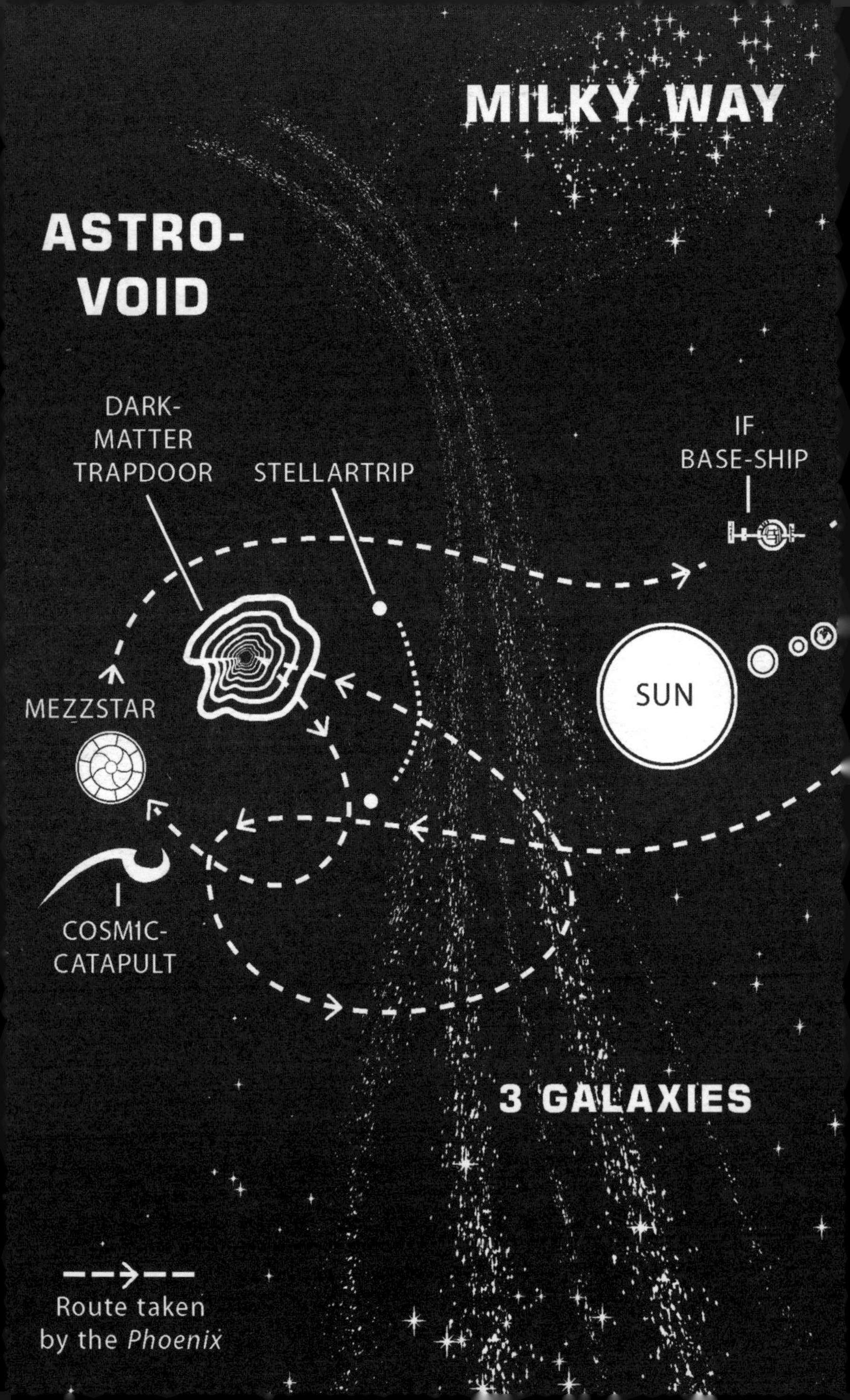
MILKY WAY
ASTRO-
VOID
DARK-
MATTER
TRAPDOOR
STELLARTRIP
IF
BASE-SHIP
SUN
MEZZSTAR
COSMIC-
CATAPULT
3 GALAXIES
Route taken
by the *Phoenix*

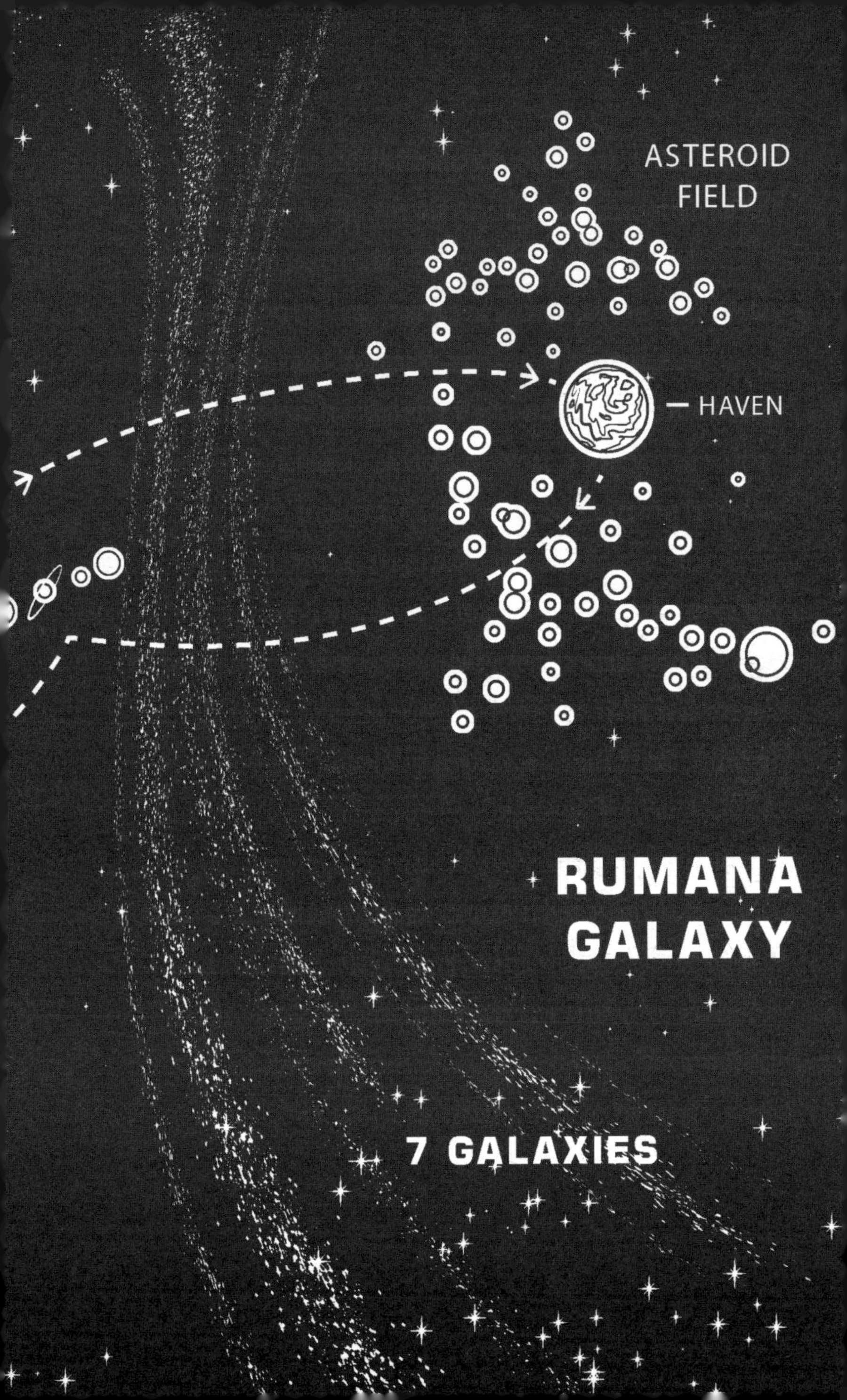
ASTEROID
FIELD
HAVEN
RUMANA
GALAXY
7 GALAXIES

STAR FIGHTERS

An elite fighting team sworn to protect and defend the galaxy

It is the year 5012 and the Milky Way galaxy is under attack . . .

After the Universal War . . . a war that almost brought about the destruction of every known universe . . . the planets in the Milky Way banded together to create the Intergalactic Force – an elite fighting team sworn to protect and defend the galaxy.

Only the brightest and most promising students are accepted into the Intergalactic Force Academy, and only the very best cadets reach the highest of their ranks and become . . .

STAR FIGHTERS

To be a Star Fighter is to dedicate your life to one mission: *Peace in Space*. They are given the coolest weapons, the fastest spaceships – and the most dangerous missions. Everyone at the Intergalactic Force Academy wants to be a Star Fighter someday.

Do YOU have what it takes?

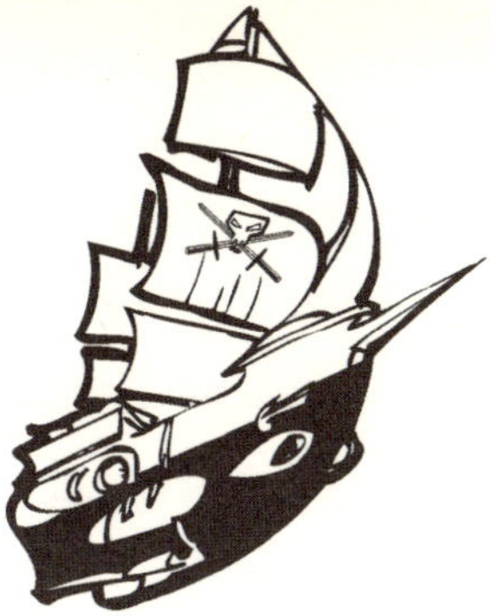

Chapter 1

'Daxx is escaping!' Peri shouted as the *Space Wolf* blazed away from the *Phoenix*.

The space pirates' vessel had every solar-wind sail unfurled like an ancient galleon. The skull-and-crossed-swords flag, the Cranky Roger, streamed behind the ship. Daxx had stolen the Heart of Mars and planned to use it in a secret weapon that could threaten the entire galaxy. It was the Star Fighters' mission to get the priceless gem back.

Peri smacked on the emergency boosters. 'We need more speed!' he shouted.

The g-force knocked Diesel to the floor as the *Phoenix* surged forward, but the half-Martian scrambled up and pushed past Otto to reach the gunnery station.

'Where's Jaxx?' Peri asked, scanning the Bridge.

Jaxx was the IF's Space Enemy Number One. They had captured him when he had nearly crash-landed on Saturn only to find out he was Selene's father. She was sure he was innocent, and that his identical twin brother, Daxx, was the real space pirate.

'I sent my dad to Engineering to try and improve the plasma flow to the thrusters,' Selene said, checking over the engineer's console. 'If anyone can make us go faster, my dad can!'

Without warning, Daxx's ship plunged towards a fiery red dwarf star.

'What on Mars is he doing?' Peri said, twisting the Nav-wheel and diving after the *Space Wolf*.

'Perhaps he's using the star's gravity field to slow us down,' Diesel suggested.

Gravity! The word lit up a bionic circuit in Peri's head. 'No, he's going to use the gravity field like a slingshot, to catapult his ship even faster out the other side of the star.'

The gauges on the control panel went haywire as they got closer to the star. The *Phoenix* began to shake. Peri knew their ship would be pulled apart and they'd be burnt alive if they got too close. But if they were too far away, they wouldn't be able to swing round the star fast enough to catch up with Daxx.

Peri watched as the space pirates' ship caught the gravitational pull of the dwarf star and zoomed away. Daxx had timed it perfectly. Now it was Peri's turn. He gripped the Nav-wheel and yanked the thrusters to 'Max'.

Shhhwoooosh! The *Phoenix* whipped round the dying star. It shot them after Daxx's ship at astonishing speed. They hurtled through entire solar systems in the blink of an eye, right on the space pirates' tail.

Fssssshhhhwooor! They skimmed past a planet, narrowly missing two moons.

'*Dung y'r'ah!*' Diesel gasped. 'That was cosmic-close!'

Peri dodged left and right, copying Daxx's moves. His brain buzzed with excitement. It wouldn't be long before Daxx would have to stop – then they would swoop down and bring him to justice.

Narrrooa! They slipped past comets and asteroids.

Suddenly, Daxx zigzagged and whipped sharply to the right.

'He's making evasive manoeuvres!' Peri yelled as the *Phoenix* zipped past Daxx's ship and watched it vanish into clouds of yellow-grey space-fog.

Peri slammed on the turbo-reverse. Instantly, the *Phoenix* spun round and shot into the cloud after Daxx. A thick mist folded around the ship.

'I'm tracking him on the Velocity View,' said Peri.

'I love a good chase!' Otto boomed. The Meigwor bounty hunter paced the Bridge excitedly.

'Does Daxx know we're following him?' Diesel asked.

'Dad and I made sure the *Phoenix*'s cloak is set at one hundred per cent efficiency,' Selene said. 'The *Space Wolf* doesn't have powerful enough sensors to detect us.'

The Bridge lights dimmed and glowed

red. '*Cosmic turbulence ahead*,' announced the calm voice of the ship's computer.

An astro-harness snaked around Peri. His stomach lurched as the *Phoenix* plunged into a patch of turbulence. The floating control panel flipped away from his grasp. Peri grabbed it with his fingertips and hauled it back as the *Phoenix* was buffeted by the space-fog.

'*Frrr'wowoh!*' Otto screamed as he was thrown into the air, bounced against the ceiling and then slammed against the deck. '*Ooooph!*' The Meigwor used his long arms to grab hold of the control panel. He stared at Peri. 'Blast the space pirates! Then we can get out of here!'

'No!' Diesel cried. 'We need the Heart of Mars in one piece to lift the curse on my planet.'

'Who cares about that stupid jewel?' Selene

snapped. 'I need Daxx alive to clear my dad's name. The IF needs proof that it's Daxx who's the real space pirate!'

'Hold on tight!' Peri yelled as the *Phoenix* burst from the nebula cloud. They were only seconds behind Daxx, but their target had changed direction again. He was swerving around the wreck of a plasma-tanker. Peri dodged between the corroded metal ribs of the tanker's hull and shot out the other side. *We're catching him!*

Red lights flashed across the control panel, but it wasn't another space-hazard. It was something potentially worse – an incoming message from the IF Command Centre.

'Otto, Selene – hide!' Peri shouted. The IF didn't know anything about Otto and Selene being aboard the *Phoenix*. If they did, Peri and Diesel would be in serious galactic trouble.

Otto raced across the Bridge and slid behind the gunnery station, but Selene wasn't as fast. Diesel pushed her to the floor.

'Lie flat and keep quiet,' the half-Martian hissed as the 360-monitor whirled up, showing the tired face of General Pegg.

'I will not keep quiet!' The general glared at Diesel. 'Star Fighters – report on your mission progress,' he barked.

'Sir –' Peri started.

'I've checked your Mission Capsule coordinates,' the general interrupted. 'Your objective was to capture Jaxx. What are you doing on that side of the universe?'

'We're hot on the heels of the pirate who stole the Heart of Mars,' Peri replied.

The general took a sharp breath. 'I hope you know what you're doing. You're heading straight for an Astro-Void.'

Peri frowned. Apart from Daxx's ship,

there was nothing at all on the 360-monitor in front of them. Peri wondered what the general was talking about. 'Sir?'

'An Astro-Void, Peri,' the general snapped. 'Diesel, you took astro-navigation classes – explain it to him.'

'I got top marks in my class, but I don't think we covered . . .' Diesel looked at Peri for support, but Peri just shrugged.

There was a tiny cough from below and they both looked down. Silently Selene put her hands together, then opened them out as wide as she could.

Diesel shook his head. 'What the *prrrip'chiq* does that mean?' the gunner muttered.

Selene rolled her eyes. 'It's a vast dark space between galaxies,' she whispered.

'What's going on?' General Pegg's eyes bulged. 'Who else is on your ship?'

Peri's throat tightened. General Pegg was

going to confiscate their Star Fighter badges for hiding Selene on board, but they couldn't pretend she wasn't there now. Peri reached down and helped her stand up. 'Selene is –'

'I know who she is! She's a stowaway and a troublemaker,' the general snapped. 'I've kicked her off the IF Space Station more times than I can remember, yet somehow she always manages to return.'

Selene shrugged. 'It's not my fault that

your security systems don't work properly.'

'Quiet!' General Pegg ordered. 'I will not have civilians on an official IF mission. Lock Selene in a holding cell for her own safety – and yours. Return with her and that space pirate in custody soon, or your Star Fighter careers will be the shortest in IF history! End message.'

Peri felt stunned as the 360-monitor whirled back into the control panel. Why hadn't he explained to General Pegg that Selene was an incredible engineer and a valuable member of the crew? They couldn't afford to lose her from the *Phoenix*.

Diesel pulled out a pair of handcuffs. 'Are you going to come along quietly then?' he asked Selene.

Selene leapt back. 'You spineless creep! After all I've done to save you!'

Diesel's yellow eyes flashed. 'No one

has ever needed to save *me*, you bossy bugonaut!'

Peri jumped up and put himself between them. 'No one is arresting Selene. Diesel, give me the cuffs.'

Diesel's narrow band of hair bristled as he handed them over. 'I can't believe you're taking her side.'

'She's part of the crew,' Peri said. 'End of story.'

'Hey, Earthlings!' Otto boomed, crawling out from behind the gunnery station. 'The cosmic-rat has led us to his nest!'

Peri turned to look where Otto was pointing. The 360-monitor showed that Daxx's vessel was heading straight for a huge shimmering blue planet.

Selene hit the intercom switch and shouted, 'Dad, come to the Bridge! You've got to see this.' Then she slammed the

'Emergency Stop' button, making the *Phoenix* come to a dead stop.

'What are you doing?' Peri demanded.

Selene put her hands on her hips. 'I don't understand. There shouldn't be any planets in an Astro-Void.'

Jaxx materialised next to Selene. He started activating the scanners.

They watched Daxx's ship duck and swerve on its approach to the shimmering blue planet as if it was flying an obstacle course.

Then the *Space Wolf* disappeared.

'He's just vanished like a plasma-phantom!' Jaxx exclaimed. 'There's no sign of cloak activation, not even a heat signature.'

Peri realised that something was horribly wrong.

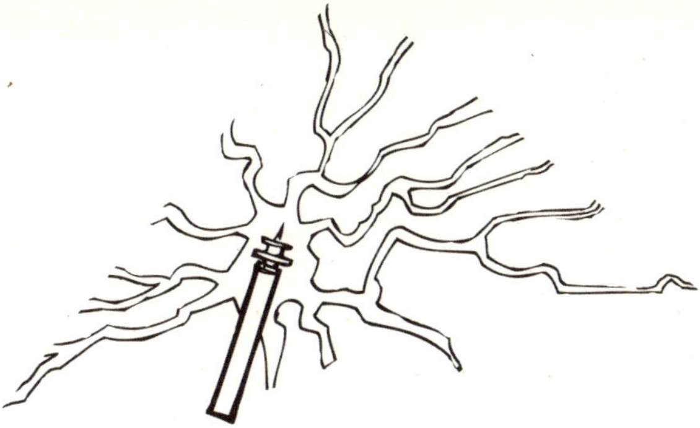

Chapter 2

'Daxx's ship can't just have disappeared. It must have landed on the blue planet,' Peri said. 'Magnify the planet, Selene. I want to see what we're up against before we get any closer.'

Selene spun a couple of zip-dials and frowned as the 360-monitor dissolved into static. 'The planet is shielded against magnified optical viewing. We'll have to get closer to see anything.'

'This is bad,' Peri said. 'First the ship we're following vanishes. Then we come across a planet that shouldn't exist. And the planet blocks our optical scans.'

'This is just like that shielded asteroid I helped us sneak on to,' Diesel said.

'You mean Haven,' Jaxx said. 'Do you think this could be another port for the Mezzoka Clan?'

Peri shivered at the idea of meeting up with the organised clan of the worst criminals in the Milky Way. He hoped that wouldn't happen.

'Your parents upgraded the Ultrawave scanner,' Selene answered. 'Let's use that to find out.'

'We're in big trouble if Daxx is working for the Mezzoka Clan.' Otto smacked a button on the gunnery station. A rectangle of red light appeared in the deck under Diesel's feet. As the gunner jumped aside, the deck panel slid away. 'Let's arm up!'

Shurrrpppt! A device like a small Ferris wheel floated up into the Bridge with more than twenty double-sided racks displaying almost every hand-held weapon Peri had ever seen – and a few that he hadn't.

'Where did that come from?' Peri gasped.

'And how does Otto know it's there when I don't?' Diesel complained. 'I'm in charge of weapons.'

'I told him about it,' Selene said. 'He organised the whole thing while we were hiding on board and you were taking your Star Fighter exams. I had to keep him occupied somehow.'

'You didn't think that telling a Meigwor bounty hunter about a huge stash of deadly weapons might be a bad idea?' Diesel pushed past Otto and hit the switch to stop the wheel rotating. He stared at the selection. 'Where are the dusters and Paralysides?'

'Dusters!' Otto boomed. 'Pathetic weapons!' He smacked the button to start the racks spinning again. 'We need much bigger firepower.'

Over on the other side of the Bridge, Peri jumped as a loud wave of static burst from the control panel. 'What the space dust was that?' he exclaimed.

'Sorry,' Selene murmured as she fiddled with a zip-dial until the noise vanished. 'I was trying to magnify the Ultrawave signal, but the planet's too well shielded. We'll try the Exo-Scanners next.'

'Reconfigure the forward sensors,' Jaxx said. 'We could use them as a plasma-sonar array. That might pick up a signal from the blue planet.'

'Good idea, Dad,' Selene said.

Otto pulled a large grey tube from the weapons rack. 'Plasma-bombs! Perfect!'

'Are you insane?' Diesel exclaimed. 'You'll blow us up if you're not careful.'

The patches around Otto's eyes darkened. 'I know what I'm doing, Martian moon-head!'

'Otto, Diesel – knock it off,' Peri ordered. 'Keep focused on our mission.'

Diesel's hair was bristling. 'I'm not the dumboid who wants to start a war with the Mezzoka Clan!'

'Who are you calling a dumboid?' Otto shouted. He pulled his silver electro-prod from his belt and flicked it out. It lengthened by a metre and began to crackle.

Peri leapt up to stop them fighting before it got out of hand, but he was too late. With a snarl, Otto lashed out at Diesel. The half-Martian dodged the electro-prod and it hit the deck. A shower of electrical

sparks exploded in front of Peri, forcing him back. Being part bionic sometimes had its downsides. *An electrical surge from the prod could fry my circuits!* He'd have to find another way to break up the fight.

Otto pointed the electro-prod at Diesel's chest. 'We need to overwhelm them with force!' he yelled.

'It's the Mezzoka Clan.' Diesel laughed. 'The whole IF couldn't overwhelm them – you'd have to obliterate the planet in one go.'

Diesel grabbed a sonic-trident from the rotating arsenal and lunged at Otto but narrowly missed. Otto swiped back with the electro-prod, but Diesel dodged it and leapt on to the Meigwor's back. Peri ran to the control panel. There was only one way to separate them now.

'Get off, space-monkey!' Otto boomed. He twisted violently. Diesel went flying across the Bridge, then he stood up, his fan of hair turning as red as a Martian sandstorm.

Peri flicked a button on the control panel. *Suurrpptt-Clunk-Clunk-Clunk-Clunk!* Diesel's Expedition Wear boots became magnetically glued to the deck, then whisked him across the floor, away from Otto, as if Diesel was skating on Saturn's ice rings.

'Enough,' said Peri.

'What are you doing?' Diesel yelled, struggling to move his feet. 'We need to sort out this weapons issue. Now is not the time to sit around chatting.'

'Diesel's right, electro-boy!' boomed Otto. 'Stay out of our debate!'

'You're both wrong,' Peri snapped. Diesel and Otto glared at him. 'We barely made it off Haven alive. If we want to find Daxx and stay in one piece, we need to use our brains this time. Selene, what can you tell me about the planet?'

'The planet's shields are still too powerful,' Selene said. 'We need to be in a close orbit to get any useful readings.'

'Isn't that a bit risky?' Peri asked.

'The *Phoenix* has the most sophisticated cloaking device in the universe,' Selene said. 'We should be able to avoid being spotted while we take pictures.'

Jaxx shook his head. 'You're forgetting that the Mezzokas' scanners will pick up anything unusual in the space-time fabric. They'll shoot first and not bother to ask questions later.'

'That's why we'll do it at speed,' said Selene. 'By the time they spot us in their sensor readings, we'll be long gone.'

'That might just work,' Jaxx said.

Peri realised this was the best idea. He

demagnetised Diesel's boots. 'Strap in. We're going to do a supersonic fly-by.'

Otto and Diesel raced to the gunnery station. Selene and Jaxx made frantic adjustments to the sensors. Peri decided that the best route to the planet was to follow Daxx's path as closely as he could.

Peri started warming up the thrusters and the main engines. His astro-harness snaked around him as his chair tilted into the flight position. 'Get ready . . . Three, two, one . . . Go!'

Peri slammed down the pyramid-shaped button and the *Phoenix* roared forward.

Eeeeeraaa! Eeeeeraaa! Sirens erupted across the Bridge. Peri saw a blur of red light hurtle at them from the Astro-Void. He tried to steer the *Phoenix* away from it, but the light was too fast.

BLAAAAAAAM! The red blur smashed

into the *Phoenix*. Peri strained against his astro-harness, while Selene and Jaxx were knocked to the floor.

'It's a cosmic-catapult!' shrieked Otto from the gunnery station.

Peri looked out of the 360-monitor. The *Phoenix* had been scooped up by a massive red laser net. Peri turned to see where the laser net was aiming. He felt a hot tingle run through all his circuits when he saw the black hole at the edge of the Astro-Void.

Chapter 3

Peri slammed on the dodge mechanism and yanked the anti-drift levers, but the *Phoenix* simply juddered and made a terrible grinding noise. It couldn't break free from the cosmic-catapult.

'Hold on, everyone!' Peri shouted.

'We're going to die!' Otto roared as the black hole filled the 360-monitor.

Chaaaa-Boiiiiiiiiinngg! The catapult flung the *Phoenix* past the black hole and out of the Astro-Void at unbelievable speed. Peri pulled the Nav-wheel, but nothing happened. He yanked more levers and slammed more buttons, but he couldn't regain control of the ship. At least the UpRighter mechanism was keeping the Bridge stable as the rest of the ship spun.

'Look out!' Selene shouted, pointing at the 360-monitor. 'Moon!'

The *Phoenix* was on a collision course with a huge chunk of rock. It would have been too late to avoid a direct hit even if they had had control of the navigation systems.

'Full power to the shields!' Peri yelled as his astro-harness tightened again. 'Brace yourselves!'

Slaaaam-Boooiiinnng! The *Phoenix* smacked into the moon, but the ship's shields flexed and tossed the ship back out into space. The whole Bridge lurched as the UpRighter mechanism failed.

Suddenly, the ceiling was below them,

then above them, and then off to the side. Peri was thrown against his astro-harness. The Bridge and the 360-monitor spun wildly in different directions. He clutched his stomach and groaned. He had never felt so space-sick before.

An astro-bucket sprung from the arm of his chair and Peri grabbed it. He glanced at the rows of swirling metal teeth inside that would chew anything up if he puked. He looked away, trying to take his mind off his space-sickness. As the ship spun, Selene and her dad held on to Peri's chair and each other while space-wrenches flew out of her pockets.

Crrraaasssh-Boiiinnng! The ship ricocheted off an asteroid, then rebounded off a comet before zipping across a planet's atmosphere and spinning away in a new direction. Only the *Phoenix*'s defence systems were keeping Peri and the crew from being smashed to pieces.

Groans were coming from the gunners' chairs. Diesel had his head buried in an astro-bucket. Peri could just see his limp green hair plastered against his head, blue sweat dripping off it. 'Make it stop,' he moaned, his voice echoing from the bucket.

Peri's stomach churned as the *Phoenix* flipped and bounced through space. He pressed his hand over his mouth and wished his bionic circuits could prevent him feeling sick.

With a jolt, the UpRighter mechanism started working again and the Bridge stopped spinning. The drone of the engines became less urgent and Peri realised that the *Phoenix*'s speed was decreasing. The ship bounced gently off another asteroid and came to a halt.

Diesel lifted his head from the astro-bucket and looked around. 'Where are we?'

The half-Martian gulped and tried to put his hand over his mouth, but he was too late. His neon-green vomit splattered into the astro-bucket. *Whirrrrrrrr!* The bucket whizzed into action.

Peri didn't want to see any more of that! He punched a button on the control panel and a map appeared on the 360-monitor. 'I can't believe it – we're half a galaxy from our last position!' He placed his palm on the smooth red section of the control panel. *Click.* It slid open and he punched in the coordinates. 'Stand by! I'm going to use Superluminal to get back to where we started.'

Peri flicked the switch. The *Phoenix* leapt forward faster than the speed of light. It was a smoother ride than their catapult-fuelled trip halfway across the galaxy. The *Phoenix* dropped out of Superluminal speed to reveal the vast emptiness of the Astro-Void.

The blue planet was gone.

'It's not here,' Otto boomed. 'You've made a mistake!'

Peri rechecked the coordinates. 'It was definitely here . . . But now it isn't.'

Diesel pulled his head free of the astro-bucket and wiped his mouth. 'How can you lose an entire planet?'

Peri glanced at Selene and Jaxx to see what they thought. Jaxx was standing up and dusting himself off while Selene sat slumped on the floor, smirking.

Peri narrowed his eyes. 'Something funny?' he asked. 'We've just lost our only lead to clear your dad's name!'

Selene's grin got wider. 'Who said we've lost the planet?'

'For Neptune's sake,' Diesel yelled. 'It doesn't take a wastoid to look outside and see that the planet is GONE!'

Selene rolled her eyes. 'You don't get planets in an Astro-Void,' she said. 'So whoever owns that planet must have fitted it with engines and flown it here –'

'Which means,' Jaxx interrupted, 'that they can probably move it wherever they like.'

'Genius,' Diesel said sarcastically. 'But *we* still don't know where it's gone.'

Selene smiled again. 'As soon as I realised it was mobile, I used a hypodermic laser to inject a tracking device into the planet's stratosphere.'

Jaxx helped his daughter up and gave her a hug. 'Smart thinking! I'm very impressed.'

Selene's hands moved over the engineer's console and made adjustments to the tracing scanners. 'It only has a range of one light year, but it should be enough to track down the planet.'

Zeeeeeee-Zaaaa-Ping!

A bright orange light beam appeared on the 360-monitor. '*Tracking the signal,*' the ship announced. The light began to snake across the Astro-Void, swirling and dipping through the emptiness. Then it stopped and the line faded away, leaving a bright orange dot on the screen.

Selene pointed. 'There! One missing planet found.'

'Space-tastic, Selene!' Peri cheered. 'Now let's go and arrest Daxx.'

Peri blasted the *Phoenix* towards the planet while everyone kept their eyes on the sensors to make sure they steered well clear of the cosmic-catapult this time around.

The shimmering blue planet appeared on their 360-monitor again.

'Diesel, Otto,' Peri said, 'let's make sure we're ready for anything they can –'

Before Peri had finished giving the order, he saw a flash of sparkling blue ahead of the *Phoenix* and another siren erupted. *Eeeaarraaa!*

Peri shielded his eyes as all the lights on the Bridge glowed bright red.

'We're slowing down,' Selene reported.

Peri pulled at the thrusters. 'How is that even possible? All the engines are running at maximum thrust.'

The black patches around Otto's eyes

turned a ghostly shade of grey and he started murmuring in a low voice. '*Ra-cnar, fagh, marigngh, fro-fulra, duphrfrig, ghirfight! Fagh.*'

'Is Otto praying?' Diesel gasped. 'I thought Meigwors weren't afraid of anything.'

Otto strapped himself in the nearest chair and shook his head. 'We're only afraid when we're going to die in the most painful way in the universe!' he boomed. 'You've just hit a StellarTrip! There is no escape!'

Chapter 4

'What is a StellarTrip, Otto?' Peri asked.

'You space-monkeys know nothing!' Otto boomed. 'It holds a string of stars together. When something crosses the wire, it pulls all the stars towards the centre of the trap! We're going to be blown apart! There won't even be space dust left.'

Peri magnified the wire on the 360-monitor and followed it along its entire length. A thin purple laser-wire stretched around the ship and then out into deep space. Otto was right – the wire was threaded through hundreds of small but powerful stars. The ends of the wire folded towards them, smashing the stars together to create the deadliest fireworks display in the universe. As more stars were caught up in the explosion, the fireball swinging towards the *Phoenix* grew larger and larger.

We've got to outrun this, Peri thought, slamming on the turbo-reverse.

The *Phoenix* responded with full power. Peri rammed the backward thrusters to 'Maximum'. The Bridge shook as the ship gave it everything it had. *Chrrorrrraarr!* The engines screamed with effort, but nothing happened.

'Stop it!' Selene yelled. 'You'll strip the plasma-flux relays and destroy the engines!'

Peri released the thrusters and the engines fell silent. Glancing at the 360-monitor, he realised his manoeuvres had just tangled the laser-wire even more closely around the ship. 'If we can't escape the wire we have to break it.'

'I have an idea.' Selene started twisting a row of zip-dials. 'Remember when we saved those moon-bats?'

Peri nodded. 'We adjusted our hand-held lasers to shoot ice-beams.'

'Exactly – we can use our laser array to make the wire cold enough to snap.' Selene punched a series of buttons.

On her command, Otto and Diesel opened fire. Bright blue beams burst from the *Phoenix* and struck the StellarTrip.

'It's not working,' Diesel reported. 'They need to be colder.'

'I'm on it!' Selene said, making more adjustments to the laser controls.

Peri ran a scan. The beams had now

dropped to the coldest temperature possible. He could see ice forming around the ship's laser ports, but none on the laser-wire. The StellarTrip had been cooled, but only enough to slow down the stars crashing towards the *Phoenix*.

'It hasn't weakened the wire, but it has bought us more time.' Peri swept his gaze across the control panel. His eyes stopped on the strange twisted button at the far end.

The Red Helix.

Peri reached for the button, then froze. His parents had warned him to use it only as a last resort. *Is this the right time?* he asked himself. This was a life or death situation – he needed to save his crew and the *Phoenix* – but the Red Helix was completely dark, unlike the Blue Helix, which had glowed when it was the right time to use it. An aching prickle flowed through his

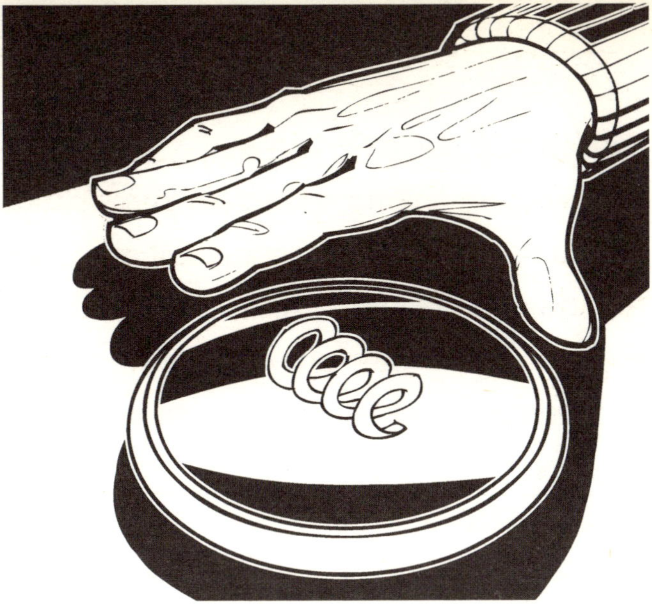

muscles. His bionic body was telling him, *Not now.*

Peri pulled his hand away. If his bionic connection with the ship didn't want him to press the Red Helix, what else could he do? The explosive fireball was getting larger and hotter with every nanometre as it got closer to the ship. Peri could see it without magnification now. They didn't stand a chance against its awesome power.

Help us, Phoenix*!*

A tingling feeling spread up Peri's hands and arms. At first he thought it was fear, but then he realised that the *Phoenix* was trying to send him a message. He took a deep breath and listened to the ship, but what he heard didn't make sense at all.

Big . . . Think.

Peri took another breath, trying not to panic. *Concentrate,* he told himself.

Think Big!

His eyes drifted towards the Expansion Pack controls. His fingers twitched, wanting to activate them.

But how can they help? Peri wondered. *They only make the* Phoenix *bigger, which would mean we'd be too bulky to fly fast . . .*

'That's it!' Peri exclaimed. If they made the ship bigger, then maybe the StellarTrip laser-wire that was tightening around them would be stretched to breaking point. They could snap it and escape!

Peri started flicking the switches to expand the ship. The ship's plan on the control panel glowed as the *Phoenix* was transformed. *Schurrrpt!* The ship gained algae-growing generators and swimming pools. Peri pressed more buttons to add a solar-sampler unit, fully functioning astro-labs and a gymnasium. The *Phoenix* was now one hundred times bigger, but Peri activated even more Expansion Packs. Firing ranges, manufacturing rooms and moon-buggy racing tracks appeared on the plan. The display of corridors and compartments was dazzling.

The tangled laser-wire contracted tighter, but the *Phoenix* kept on growing. Peri pushed the last Expansion Pack button. The ship reached its maximum capacity.

Ting-ting! Peri and his crew stood still as they listened to the strange noise echoing through the Bridge. *Ting-ting-ting-ting!* It sounded like the laser-wire was stretching. *Ting-ting-ting!* The *Phoenix* shuddered under the strain. *TING-PING-PING!*

KRRRAAACCCKKKK! Peri covered his ears as an almighty noise ripped through the Bridge. He gripped the control panel to steady himself as the ship shook. Peri saw the laser-wire recoil into the Astro-Void. The StellarTrip had snapped and was throwing stars spiralling off into space.

Peri and the others cheered, but the sound was drowned out by the howling of sirens. Angry red letters flashed across the 360-monitor: *Hazard Alert!* He checked the scanners. Part of the StellarTrip was spinning towards the *Phoenix* on a collision course!

Peri slammed a button to collapse all the Expansion Packs, which vanished in seconds.

'Let's go,' he said, smacking the pyramid-shaped button to activate the engines.

As the ship shunted forward, Diesel yelled, 'Peri! Port side!'

On Peri's left, a gigantic snake-like whip of laser-wire and exploding stars was smashing towards the *Phoenix*.

Peri slammed on the dodge mechanism, sending the *Phoenix* sliding sideways to starboard. The snake of stars swept harmlessly past.

'Hold on,' Peri yelled as the stars spun around to strike again. He yanked the Nav-wheel hard. The *Phoenix* swept up and around as the StellarTrip sliced close to one side, then the other.

There's no way to outrun it, he realised.

There was only one option left. He'd

have to turn the whip's power against itself.

'What are you doing?' Diesel and Otto shrieked in horror, as Peri turned the *Phoenix* in the direction of the StellarTrip.

'Trust me!' Peri yelled. As the fiery whip curled up and lashed out, he yanked down the thrusters. The *Phoenix* soared ahead, pulling the whip along in their space-wake. Peri turned and twisted the Nav-wheel, sending the ship in a wide loop and setting the whip on a collision course with itself, then he jerked the ship straight up and out of the way.

Shaannaa-baaaam! The whip snapped, tearing itself apart, sending stars flying off in all directions.

'*Mars'rakk!*' Diesel cheered as he high-fived Peri.

Behind them, Selene and Jaxx were punching the air.

But Otto was staring up at the 360-monitor. Peri could tell from the look on the Meigwor's face that they weren't out of trouble yet.

Chapter 5

'There's another trap!' Otto boomed.

Peri turned to look, but all he could see between the *Phoenix* and the shimmering blue planet was blackness. He slammed on the turbo-brakes and brought their ship to a complete halt. 'What do you mean there's another trap, Otto?'

'We're in deadly trouble!' Otto said. 'It's a dark-matter trapdoor!'

'I don't see anything,' Diesel scoffed.

Otto flicked his black tongue towards Diesel's face. 'It's made of *dark matter*! It wouldn't be a very good trap if it was visible to the eyes of inferior life forms!'

'But the Exo-Scanner should detect it,' Selene said. She twisted a zip-dial and a monitor whirled from the control panel. The thermal image of the area revealed nothing. 'Are you *sure* there's something there, Otto? I've adjusted the wavelength range, but there's no sign of anything.'

'Isn't that proof enough?' Otto boomed. 'Whoever owns that planet wants to keep unwanted visitors out! They've used a cosmic-catapult and a StellarTrip! A dark-matter trapdoor must be next!'

Peri stared into the darkness ahead of him. They hadn't spotted either of the other space-hazards until it was too late. 'I guess it makes sense . . . What do dark-matter trapdoors do, Otto?'

'Nobody knows,' Otto said, 'because nobody has lived to tell.'

Peri clenched his fist in frustration. They were so close to completing their mission. All they needed to do was slip past the trap, then they could find and arrest Daxx and recover the Heart of Mars. He wished he could be in two places at once so he could trigger the trap without endangering the *Phoenix*.

The artery in his neck started throbbing, but it wasn't his heart racing or his blood pressure increasing. It felt urgent, like a flashing button on the control panel but inside him. His bionic half was sending him a message.

Peri raised his fingers to his neck. He could feel blood beating under his fingertips, and behind the artery he could feel something else. A small button.

He pushed it. *Click!*

Body Duplication activated, announced a voice in his head. *Imagine secondary location.*

Peri pictured himself on a mini-pod racing towards the blue planet. A blinding flash of light burst through his mind like a solar-flare. Suddenly, he was sliding down a long silver tube into a mini-pod, but part of him was still on the Bridge. His mind strained with astonishment. *I'm in two places at once!*

He landed in a mini-pod with a *hurrrupt.* An astro-harness snaked around his body. He took a deep breath while he tried to understand what was happening. He could feel and touch the mini-pod as if his body was normal, but he was also aware of the part of him he had left behind on the Bridge. It felt like he'd left behind an energy shell that was able to see and hear what was

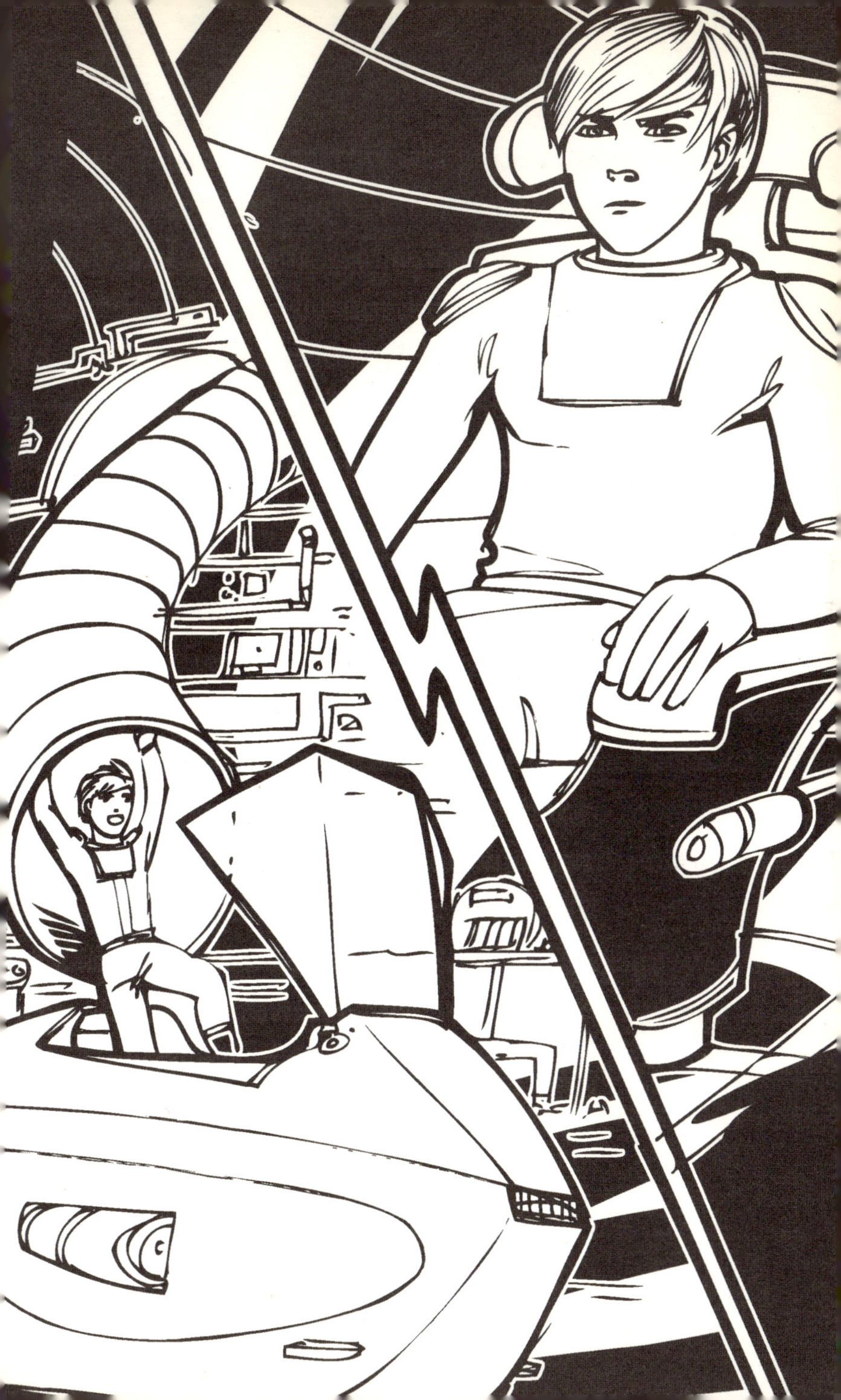

happening, but was fixed to the spot, as still as a statue. The shell-Peri on the Bridge could not move or even speak.

Peri's pod-self fired up the mini-pod's engines and blasted towards the dark-matter trapdoor.

He became aware that, back on the Bridge, Selene was yelling at his energy shell. 'You reckless idiot! I don't know how you did it, but I know you've split yourself in half. Even split in half, you still have a heat signature.'

Peri's pod-self hit the control panel to activate the com-unit. 'This is going to work. Just keep watching the Exo-Scanner and record how big the trap is.'

As the mini-pod glided through the blackness, Peri could feel sweat trickling down his neck. His Expedition Wear suddenly felt stifling. At any moment the trap was going to spring into action. He placed his thumbs over the emergency-reverse thrusters so he'd be ready to escape.

Caaarraaaroorraar! The space around him was ripped apart by a dark red light. Instantly, the mini-pod lurched forward. Being sucked into the dark-matter trapdoor was like being pulled into the jaws of the largest cosmic killer whale in the universe.

Peri slammed on the emergency-reverse thrusters, but nothing could escape the overwhelming force of the trapdoor. The straps of astro-harness cut into his chest – the dark matter was trying to rip him right out of the mini-pod!

He punched the controls again, trying to get the pod away from the trapdoor, but nothing worked. Instead he was spinning into the trapdoor's jaws. *There's no way I can fly the mini-pod out of here,* he realised. *I've got to use my bionic connection to escape.*

As he tried to lift his hand to his neck, Peri realised that the gravitational pull of the dark matter made his hand weigh more than his entire body – and it was getting heavier every second. It felt like the trapdoor was trying to rip his hand from his wrist.

Activate Fight-or-Flight, he shouted in his mind.

Energy buzzed through Peri's body as his muscles swelled. He fought against the pull of the dark matter, dragging his hand slowly up to his neck. But even with superhuman strength it wasn't easy. His whole body was screaming with pain. He clenched his eyes shut and reached for the hidden button.

Click!

Peri didn't know if it was too late. It felt like the black hole was ripping him apart, like his muscles were being torn from his bones and his circuits were melting.

Then there was a blinding flash and the pain vanished.

Peri opened his eyes. He was standing on the Bridge, surrounded by Selene, Jaxx, Otto and Diesel.

I'm alive! he thought, taking a step forward and smiling at his friends.

'That was easy,' he said, just before his legs collapsed under him and he was plunged into darkness.

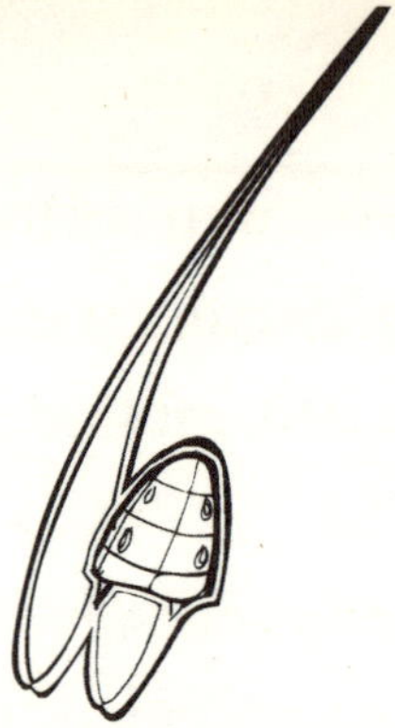

Chapter 6

Peri felt as if he'd been stretched between two moons. Every muscle in his body ached and his head was pounding, but his energy levels had regenerated back to normal. He opened his eyes and found himself in the captain's chair.

'Is everyone OK?' he asked.

'Did you have a good nap?' Diesel replied. 'What a wastoid, sleeping on a mission.'

'Hey, I almost burnt out my circuits,' Peri snapped. *Another argument won't help anything,* he told himself, taking a deep breath. 'Did we get what we needed?'

'Yes, thanks to your crazy manoeuvre,' Selene said. 'I've never seen anything so recklessly brave. We were able to chart the dimensions of the trapdoor and pilot around it. But we were waiting for you to recover before we approached the planet.'

'Great! Let's go and get Daxx,' Peri said. He clicked his fingers and the control panel slid over to him. 'Selene, set the cloak to "Max".'

Peri plotted a course to avoid a string of defensive satellites between them and the shimmering planet. 'Diesel, Otto – be on alert! But don't activate weapons until I say.'

Peri's fingers automatically twisted a zip-dial marked 'Ultra-Stealth thrusters'. He turned it to 'Maximum' and pulled the lever all the way down. The *Phoenix* roared towards the planet, but the Bridge's lights turned red and started flashing.

'*This is the MezzStar,*' a voice boomed over a radio channel. '*Surrender peacefully or die.*'

Peri brought the ship to a halt.

Jaxx put a protective arm around Selene. 'This is very bad! I've heard such horrible stories about what happens on the MezzStar. It's a planet created and owned by the Mezzoka Clan. It's their secret headquarters. If Daxx flew here, he must be working with them. We'd better surrender.'

Peri shivered and opened a com-channel. 'This is the *Phoenix*. We are surrendering peacefully.'

A red laser shot up from the MezzStar. '*Follow the laser to your landing bay or be destroyed.*'

Peri followed the red light. As they got closer, he realised that the MezzStar was not actually a planet – it was a massive space-base. One side had been scooped out and resembled a giant dish. At its centre was a transparent dome that stared at them like a giant eye. Parked in rows around the sides of the dish were colossal flying rubbish-trucks with large pincers.

'Why are there so many dump-jets?' he asked.

'The Mezzoka Clan use space-rubbish collection as a cover for their criminal activities,' Jaxx replied.

'So the MezzStar is the centre of their entire intergalactic criminal operation?' Peri said as he guided the *Phoenix* into a parking slot between the dump-jets.

Jaxx nodded. 'The Mezzokas are the most organised and vicious criminals in the universe. We must proceed cautiously.'

Diesel started activating drawers from

under his gunnery station. 'Where's my Eterni-chew?'

Peri frowned. 'You're worried about chewing gum at a time like this?!'

Diesel pointed at the dump-jets. 'This place must be a garbage collection centre for the whole universe. It's going to smell awful.'

As the *Phoenix* stopped, a voice boomed over the radio channel, '*Leave your ship immediately. No weapons allowed.*'

'Otto,' Peri said, 'hand over your weapons.'

The patches around Otto's eyes darkened as he shook his head. 'I'd rather die than have fewer than six weapons on me!'

'You'll put us all in danger if you don't leave them behind,' Peri said. 'The Mezzokas don't look like they need an excuse to be nasty.'

Otto pulled several silver batons, two blasters and a string of grenades from his belt and dropped them with a *clang-clang-clang!* Then he pulled a twelve-barrelled space-laser from a place Peri couldn't figure out.

'Thank you,' Peri said, leading them to the exit. He opened the door and saw a dozen Mezzokan guards lined up in rows to meet them. They were all as tall as Otto and just as well-built and bulky. But each guard had three eyes and two extra arms.

‘Halt!’ they announced as one. ‘We search you for weapons.’

Two guards grabbed Peri and eight hands patted down his Expedition Wear. They took chocolate spacebars and card keys from his pocket and kept them.

‘Hey,’ Peri protested. ‘They’re not weapons!’

‘We don’t know that,’ one of the guards replied. ‘Those spacebars could be poison.’

Peri grabbed for the spacebars and card keys. He glanced at the others. Selene was trying to reclaim a space-wrench and a pad of sticky notes. Other guards were shoving Otto while Diesel was wrestling for his pack of Eterni-chew.

The *Phoenix* crew eventually surrendered their belongings. Diesel huffed and puffed in frustration while Otto stood with his double-jointed arms folded around him.

'Follow us,' the guards said. 'The boss wants to see you.'

They were marched through the corridors of the MezzStar. Another hand slipped over Peri's shoulder. He swatted it away before it could pinch his Star Fighter badge. He glanced behind him to see the others struggling against the guards' pick-pocketing. It was as if the guards couldn't help stealing and, with so many hands, they were natural-born thieves.

Finally, the *Phoenix* crew and the guards reached a pair of jewel-encrusted gold doors, which swung open to reveal a massive hall. A laser fountain in the middle of the room sent ripples of light across the hand-painted ceiling. Priceless works of art hung on the walls.

Diesel gasped. 'That's one of my father's paintings, *The Martian Lisa*! It's been missing for years. The Mezzokas must have stol—' Peri elbowed Diesel in the side. 'What was that for, voidoid?'

'Be careful what you say,' Peri hissed. 'We're in enough trouble without accusing them of stealing.'

Peri glanced down to the far end of the room. A muscular alien with extra-large ears sat on a throne made of gold bricks. He had two forearms jutting out from each elbow and hands where his feet should have been.

The guards pushed the Star Fighters towards the alien. In the reflection of the gold throne, Peri noticed that the alien had an eye in the back of his head, which he used to look up at a screen behind him.

A green face flashed up on to the screen and the alien shouted, 'No.' Just before the screen went black, the green face became a mask of fear.

The alien on the throne focused his two front eyes on the *Phoenix* crew. 'Welcome, Peri, Diesel and Selene. I am sorry for the trouble we put you through, Jaxx.'

Behind him on the monitor, another alien face flickered into view. It was pale blue, and had two rows of eyes that were all filled with tears.

'Maybe!' snarled the muscular alien. The many eyes on the blue face lit up with relief. The screen went black again, and their 'host' continued in his normal voice. 'Otto . . . a bounty hunter whose reputation goes before him! Welcome to my humble planet.'

Peri frowned. Whoever this alien was, he knew more about them than they did about him – and Peri didn't like that. 'I'm sorry,' Peri said. 'But who might you be?'

The alien laughed, a low sinister laugh. 'I am Tonka Mezzoka, head of the Mezzoka Clan. And I'm going to make you an offer you can't refuse.'

Chapter 7

Tonka smiled at Peri. 'The *Phoenix* is the only ship to have made it through my sophisticated booby traps. Imagine what I could do with such a fabulous vessel! But the *Phoenix* is useless without you, Peri. If you and your crew come and work for me, I'll let you live.'

Another face appeared on the screen behind him. This one was as white as a summer cloud on Earth, and it had two mouths, one in each cheek. Both sets of teeth were chattering in terror.

The eye in the back of Tonka's head swivelled up to look at the latest face. 'Yes,' he shouted. The white alien's two mouths grinned broadly as the screen went black once more.

'I can always use a smart spaceman,' Tonka said to Peri.

'And if we don't agree to work for you?' Peri asked.

'Then you'll be as useful as trash.' The Mezzoka Clan boss pressed a button on the throne and a giant screen appeared above him. It showed a yellow-skinned alien strapped into a firing tube. 'And trash . . . gets flung into space.'

Peri felt his throat tighten as he realised what the clan boss was about to do.

'No!' Tonka shouted.

The yellow alien screamed. This time the screen did not go black. Tonka made sure that Peri and the others could see the helpless yellow alien being fired into outer space.

Then Tonka continued talking to Peri, as if none of it had happened. 'If you refuse, you and your ship will be destroyed. The choice is yours entirely.'

If we're to have any chance of surviving, Peri thought, *we have to agree to work with him . . . or at least pretend to.* He glanced at his crew, and

hoped that they would go along with his plan.

Peri took a deep breath. 'You make a convincing argument. We'll agree, but can we ask one favour?'

Tonka narrowed his eyes. 'What?'

'We've heard that you've created a massive super-weapon greater than any in the galaxy,' Peri said. 'We were hoping to see it for ourselves. It would be good to know exactly how powerful our new boss is.'

Tonka clapped his four hands and two feet-hands together. 'Excellent! You'll find the Mezzanator truly inspiring! I promise you, you've never seen such an amazing weapon. I'm itching to test it and see it in action. I've just had the final segment delivered, but then, you already know that.' He stood on his feet-hands. 'Follow me.'

Tonka turned and walked through a door

behind his throne. The guards pressed in against Peri and the rest of the crew, marching them to the end of the massive hall. They followed Tonka down a series of corridors until they reached what looked like a planetarium. Peri gazed up through the thick glass dome ceiling. They were at the bottom of the vast landing bay. He could see the *Phoenix* parked among the thousands of dump-jets.

In the centre of the room was what Peri guessed was the Mezzanator. From a huge base of computers and machinery, it curved up to a crystalline point. Thick black tubes were wrapped like snakes around the giant weapon. Between them, huge whirling silver-bladed fans kept the circuits cool as sparks leapt from one wire to another. On three platforms linked by steep metal ladders, technicians were scrambling around, making adjustments. On the middle platform one of the technicians had a very familiar face.

'Daxx!' Selene and her father exclaimed.

The space pirate looked down and grinned. He opened a small space-case next to him and pulled out a glowing jewel as big as his hand. It sparkled with rays of yellow, orange, silver and gold as if it was alive.

The Heart of Mars, Peri realised. He grabbed Diesel's shoulder as the gunner made to charge. They watched as Daxx slotted the stone into the centre of the weapon.

Tonka clasped a pair of hands together. 'I had to kidnap experts from across the universe to build this magnificent machine. But not Daxx, of course. I didn't need to kidnap him – he was more than happy to help!'

'What do you need this weapon for?' Peri

asked. 'You're already the most powerful crime boss in the universe.'

Tonka clapped Peri on the back with two of his hands and almost sent him flying. 'There's always more power and money to be earned!' Tonka laughed. 'With the Mezzanator I can punish any galaxy that refuses to pay me protection money.'

Peri was confused. 'Protection money?'

'Galaxies pay me *not* to attack them. Now anyone who refuses to pay up will suffer the wrath of the Mezzanator.' One of Tonka's eyes narrowed and looked at Diesel. 'The Emperor of the Milky Way has repeatedly refused to give in to my requests . . .'

'My father doesn't pay protection money to criminals,' Diesel said.

'But without the Heart of Mars he's not as powerful as he used to be,' Tonka said.

'If I don't collect from the emperor, the other galaxies might think I've gone soft. They might decide not to pay me as well. You see how I'm left without a choice?'

'You could stop demanding protection money,' Selene said.

Tonka shook his head. 'Impossible. I must make an example of the Milky Way to show the entire universe what happens to any galaxy that doesn't pay up.' He waved at Daxx with three of his hands. 'Let's test the weapon.'

Technicians started slamming access panels and hurrying away from the weapon. Daxx slid down a ladder to the control panel. He pressed a button and a large screen flickered to life, showing an image of the Astro-Void. He punched another button and the Mezzanator started swivelling. *Hmmannna.* The image on the screen panned across a background of stars. *Chugggaaa.* The weapon came to a halt and zoomed in on a solar system.

'Target selected,' Daxx said. 'An uninhabited solar system called Epsilon D-5-9-0 – twelve planets, all radioactive.'

Tonka nodded, waving his hands impatiently. 'Fire!'

Daxx hit a large red button and the Mezzanator growled into action.

Shhaaaa-blaaam! A clean cold bullet of light exploded from the weapon and shot through the glass dome. It sparkled as it raced through the Astro-Void before plunging into the star at the centre of the targeted solar system.

KAAAAAA-BOOOM! The star exploded in a burst of ultra-bright light that flooded the Mezzanator room, almost blinding Peri. Even the Mezzokan guards had to cover their three eyes.

Peri was stunned. As the initial burst of light faded, the entire fabric of the solar system was ripped apart by a swirling firestorm. The burning gases collapsed inwards, leaving no trace of any of the dozen planets.

The star went supernova! Peri thought.

'No one should have a weapon this powerful!' Otto boomed. 'It takes all the fun out of battle!'

'Exactly,' Tonka said. 'Now no one will ever dare to oppose me!' He laughed, waggling all his hands.

Peri realised they had to stop this galactic criminal – before he destroyed the entire universe!

Chapter 8

A solar system of twelve planets had been completely destroyed in seconds. Tonka watched the blazing supernova, hopping about and clapping his feet-hands together. Peri saw the eye in the back of the alien's head narrow as it glanced towards him and Diesel.

'Take aim at the Milky Way!' he commanded.

'No!' Diesel shouted, lunging for Tonka. Before he had even got close, one of the guards grabbed him from behind with three hands. A fourth hand was slapped across Diesel's mouth.

Peri had a vision of himself using his bionic strength to push guards out of the way and pummel the Mezzanator into pieces before throwing Tonka off the MezzStar. His limbs tingled with excitement, but he forced himself to ignore it. They couldn't defeat the Mezzoka Clan on their own. Even with his superhuman bionic strength, they were still outnumbered. He was going to have to use his brain instead.

'Hmmm . . . Arghh!' Diesel moaned through the guard's hand as he struggled to get free.

Tonka shook his head. 'This is your father's fault, Diesel, not mine. He should have swallowed his pride and paid up. Now he's being taught a lesson none of the other galaxies will ever forget.'

Peri watched as Daxx adjusted the controls and the Mezzanator rotated. *Chugggaaa.* The image on the screen moved from the supernova across countless stars and planets. The screen filled with the swirling arms of the Milky Way.

The Mezzanator slid into place and stopped. The image came into focus. Peri caught sight of the dusty red gleam of Mars and the yellow gas giant, Jupiter.

Peri's head began to buzz with an overwhelming need to get back on board the *Phoenix*. It had to be a message from the ship. Peri tried to focus on it, but all he could see in his mind's eye was a red blur.

A trickle of cold sweat ran down his back. A blue-and-green planet was now clearly visible on the monitor. Earth. Behind it shone the bright yellow sun. Peri needed to know what the *Phoenix* wanted him to do right now. He tried to clear his mind, but the image of the red blur just wouldn't shift. It was stuck in his head like a stubborn stain. Peri wished he had a button that could make the image go away.

Peri tried not to gasp. *A button!* The *Phoenix* was telling him that the time to press the Red Helix was now!

He raised his hand to his neck, but before he could press the Body Duplication button, a guard's head swivelled towards him suspiciously. Peri swallowed and slowly lifted his hand to his head. He scratched behind his ears as the guard turned away. Without wasting another nanosecond, Peri pressed the Body Duplication button underneath his pulsing artery.

Imagine secondary location, the voice in his head instructed.

Peri pictured himself on the Bridge of the *Phoenix*. In an internal flash of light as bright as the supernova, he was split into two bodies again. His energy-shell body was trapped on the MezzStar.

His duplicated body was back on the *Phoenix*!

There wasn't much time. Peri checked through the eyes of his energy-shell body and saw Daxx arguing with Tonka about which coordinates to use in order to attack the Milky Way. As they argued, Peri raced to the *Phoenix*'s control panel. His fingers were a blur as he opened up a com-channel.

'Emergency message to IF Command!' he yelled. 'Peri reporting. Sending location of the MezzStar. Tonka Mezzoka has a deadly weapon that could destroy the entire Milky Way. Mobilise all active ships for attack and rescue. Mega priority – Code Alpha-Omega-One!'

Then Peri flipped a switch allowing him to activate an emergency com-channel to his crew. 'I've split into two,' he told them. 'I'm going to activate the Red Helix, even though I have absolutely no idea what it's going to do! We might be able to over-power Tonka in the chaos!'

Peri glanced back through the eyes of his energy-shell body. In the Mezzanator room, Tonka had just pressed the button to initiate the countdown. 'Five . . .' the Mezzoka boss shouted. 'Four . . . three . . .'

On the Bridge, the Red Helix button was now glowing with urgency. As Tonka yelled, 'Fire!', Peri slammed his hand down on it.

KAA-BOOM! A bullet of cold light shot from the Mezzanator, crackling with destructive energy. At the same time the *Phoenix* belched a huge bubble of liquid lead. *Buuurrrpptt!*

Kaaa-splosh! The giant lead blob swallowed the bullet of light.

Peri leaned forward, peering through the 360-monitor, feeling his heart beating hard and fast in his chest. This had to work – if it didn't, the Milky Way was doomed!

The giant blob expanded and contracted, ripples of lightning flashing through it. Peri hoped the lead would absorb the energy. It had to. He held his breath.

Ffffffurrrrrrrrrrrpppppp! The lead ball grew still, drifting like a balloon on a breeze. The bullet of light inside it flickered and went out.

It had been disarmed! Peri punched the air.

'You!' Peri heard Tonka scream in the Mezzanator control room.

He looked through the eyes of his energy-shell body and saw Tonka storming towards him. There was no time to lose. His energy shell wouldn't be able to defend itself. Peri raised his hand to his neck and pressed the button beneath his skin.

Instantly, he was back in his body. Selene and Diesel stood beside him.

Tonka was waving his four hands in the air and yelling at him. 'Tell me how you did it, you space-rat!'

Peri grinned, but his legs were trembling.

Activating the Body Duplication powers had drained his bionic batteries. 'I've been here the whole time,' he replied, doing his best to hold Tonka's gaze.

Tonka's eyes narrowed. 'I know you did something.'

'I can't believe it,' Daxx groaned. He hit the control panel with his fist. 'The bullet is useless now!'

Peri looked up through the dome. The shiny silver blob of metal was taking on a dull grey colour as the lead hardened around the bullet of light. Soon it would be safely trapped.

Peri shared a smile with Selene and Diesel. They had saved the galaxy – again!

Tonka started laughing. 'You think you're so smart. But the lead won't hold that amount of destructive energy for very long. As soon as it cracks the whole thing will explode. Everything around you will be destroyed – not just the MezzStar, but your friends and your precious ship.'

'Ooof!'

Peri turned and saw that Jaxx had pushed over a guard and then dodged past another Mezzoka on his way towards the door.

'Dad!' Selene yelled. She tried to run after Jaxx, but some guards grabbed her.

Jaxx glanced at Selene over his shoulder, then disappeared through the open door.

Jaxx must have a plan to save us, Peri told himself. *He wouldn't abandon us like this . . . would he?*

'Don't just stand there,' shouted Daxx. 'After him!'

'Quiet, Daxx,' Tonka yelled. 'He won't escape the MezzStar blowing up. We already knew your brother was a coward.'

'Look!' Otto boomed, pointing to someone running out into the landing bay.

Peri's circuits tingled as he willed Jaxx to head for the *Phoenix*. But instead Jaxx pulled an alien out of the nearest dump-jet and scrambled inside.

'He really is abandoning us!' Peri gasped.

After all they had done to try to prove Jaxx's innocence, *this* was how he repaid them?

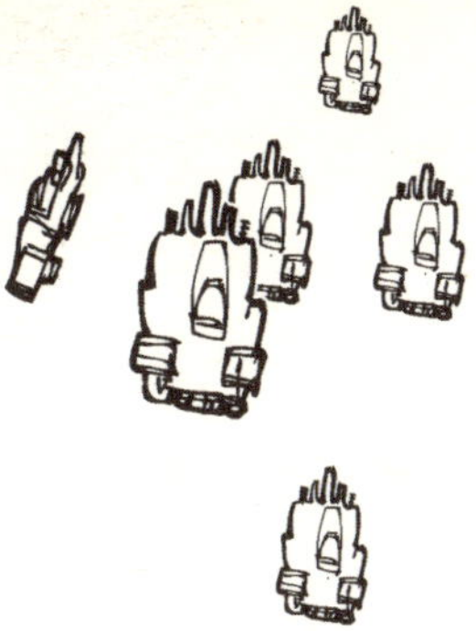

Chapter 9

Peri's mouth fell open as he watched Jaxx start up the stolen dump-jet. But rather than head out into the Astro-Void, Selene's father spun round and opened the rubbish-truck's gigantic pincers. Then he grabbed hold of the massive ball of solid lead.

'He's not fleeing!' Selene said. 'He's trying to save us all!'

Peri's body felt numb as Jaxx started to drag the ball away from the MezzStar. *How far will he get before the lead ball cracks and allows the bullet trapped inside to explode?*

'My dad's risking his life!' Selene yelled at Tonka and Daxx. 'And it's all your fault!'

Peri gasped as the dump-jet and the lead ball began spinning, whirling faster and faster, as if out of control. His heart was pounding so hard it felt like it was going to burst. Then the pincers on the dump-jet flew open and the giant lead blob was pitched away from the planet like a cosmic bowling ball.

The massive jaws of the dark-matter trapdoor opened up and swallowed the blob whole.

Crrraaacckkk-BRRAAAMMMB!

Peri and the others were thrown to the ground as a shock wave ripped through the MezzStar. The dark-matter trapdoor was torn apart by the explosion – it had absorbed most of the bullet's deadly force. Peri looked around for Jaxx's dump-jet and saw it heading back unharmed.

Neeeee-neeee. Neeee-neee. Sirens sprang into life in the Mezzanator room.

'*Ultraviolet cloaks down!*' a voice shouted over the tannoy. '*Hostile detected. Protect Tonka and the MezzStar at all costs. Action stations!*'

Across the Astro-Void, Peri could see IF ships swarming towards the Mezzokan space-base. His message had got through!

'Peace in space!' he yelled as he crouched in the cosmic-combat position.

Diesel and Otto leapt next to him.

'You're surrounded, Tonka. Surrender,' Otto boomed.

'Never!' Tonka shouted.

Ka-ka-ka! The sounds of explosions filled the air as the IF ships came within firing range of the MezzStar.

Mezzoka Clan guards sprinted into the room. 'Kill the intruders!' Tonka yelled.

'Daxx, secure the Heart of Mars and come with me!'

Peri ducked under a rushing guard's four flailing arms and chased Tonka, who was pushing his way towards the door.

Six more guards surrounded Peri, each of them levelling electro-prods. Peri panicked. The only way he could come out on top was if he somehow outnumbered them.

And then he had a crazy idea.

Peri pressed the button in his neck and imagined himself standing away from the guards.

In a flash of light, he was behind them. His energy shell was trapped by the circle of guards, but Peri kept his finger to his neck. There was another flash – and another, and another. Within seconds, a dozen Peris filled the room. If any of the guards had challenged the main energy shell they might have figured out that it was no more dangerous than a statue, but the guards were too confused by the dozen Peris surrounding them. They dropped their weapons and ran away, crying out that the 'Milky Way boy' had magical powers.

Peri scanned the chaos, searching for Tonka and Daxx. The space pirate was climbing down off the Mezzanator, while the alien crime boss was battling his way towards the door.

Peri spotted Otto and Diesel. He ducked under the nearest guard and sprinted towards them. 'Daxx mustn't escape!'

Otto seized Diesel with one arm. 'We'll catch the pirate!' he boomed.

As Otto and Diesel ran off after their prey, Peri turned to the mass of guards pouring into the room around the Mezzanator.

Somehow the other Peris were managing to fight.

Peri knew that securing the Heart of Mars before someone else stole it was his top priority. But he would need help. He looked around for Selene and saw her tackling two guards with a space-wrench.

Peri activated his superhuman Fight-or-Flight speed and dashed towards her. As he passed, he grabbed her arm and pulled her away from the guards.

'What are you doing?' she yelled as they zipped through the room towards the Mezzanator.

'We need to get the Heart of Mars!' he shouted. 'You search for it, and I'll keep the guards occupied.' Peri stopped and kicked a guard away from the front of the weapon. 'Climb!' he yelled to Selene as he let her go.

Selene scrambled up the metal steps and on to the middle platform as Peri felt his limbs getting heavy.

'I won't be able to hold them off for much longer!' he warned Selene.

'Almost there!' she shouted back.

A guard charged at him. Peri threw a one-two punch. He saw the guard fall to the floor, and felt his own legs wobble as if he had been hit over the head himself – which he had been. Countless times.

The Mezzokan guards were now attacking every version of Peri that was in the room. His ears were filled with grunts and yells, and his nose was stuffed with the smell of Mezzokan sweat and electro-prod burns. He couldn't see straight any more and his body swayed uncontrollably.

A warning screeched in his head: *Reboot system!*

But I can't stop until I know no one will be able to build another Mezzanator.

'Peri, I've got it!' Selene yelled from above.

With relief, Peri hit the button on his neck.

Snnnnaaap! Every version of himself crashed back into his body, which shook as if he was being electrocuted. He saw that

Tonka had managed to escape the crowd and was about to sneak out. Peri stepped forward to go after him, but then the ground seemed to shudder. He was close to exhaustion and dangerously weak.

There were shouts from the other side of the room. Peri turned to see IF Star Fighters storming in. Within moments they had the Mezzokan guards lying face down on the ground. The Star Fighters pulled a single metal loop from their Expedition Wear. With a flick, the loop doubled into handcuffs. They flicked them again for handcuffs that would fit the Mezzokan guards' extra wrists.

Peri fell to his knees. He was on the verge of passing out. He saw Daxx being arrested by the IF. *Otto and Diesel must have reached him in time.*

He saw Selene and Jaxx being arrested too.

I have to explain what happened, he thought desperately. *Maybe Otto can explain . . .* But when Peri looked around, he noticed that the Meigwor bounty hunter was nowhere to be seen. He had somehow slipped away!

'Wait!' Peri croaked. 'Selene and Jaxx . . . are on our side . . .'

But before he could say anything else, his vision blurred, and the whole room dissolved into blackness.

Chapter 10

Peri fiddled nervously with his titanium Star Fighter badge as he waited for the transport-tube to arrive. Almost a week had passed since the IF had stormed the MezzStar, but he hadn't been allowed to leave the Med Centre until now. He'd spent the first two days in a deep sleep while his body repaired itself, then once he was awake he'd been bombarded with hundreds of questions about the mission. But he was more interested in finding out how his crew were, and getting the chance to explain that Selene and Jaxx were on their side.

This morning General Pegg had summoned him to the Command Centre. Peri was sure he was in cosmic-size trouble.

Ping! The transport-tube arrived. *Shrrruuupt!* The doors slid open to reveal Diesel bobbing up and down on the cushioned yellow deck of the capsule. The half-Martian's narrow band of hair fanned out in a shade of royal purple.

'You were asleep the whole journey back to the base-ship. For a half-bionic boy, you're quite lazy!'

'I still helped save the galaxy,' Peri said, grinning and stepping into the transport-tube. The yellow padded floor pushed back, making him wobble.

Shrrruuupt! The transport-tube doors closed and the capsule started moving. Peri tried to wedge himself into a corner, but he kept bouncing against the cushioned walls towards Diesel.

'Have you heard anything about the others? Do you know if the IF found Otto?'

'Otto was long gone by the time the IF squad arrived,' Diesel said. Despite himself, he looked impressed by the Meigwor's cunning. 'Obviously he couldn't risk being arrested. His planet is our enemy after all.'

'Otto is the Meigwors' enemy too,' Peri pointed out. 'They think he betrayed them and sided with the Milky Way.'

'Don't worry about Otto,' said Diesel. 'He's as slippery as a space-eel! He can look after himself. Careful!' Diesel grunted, pushing Peri away as they collided with each other in the bouncy transport-tube.

With a low hum, the transport-tube came to a stop. The doors slid open and they tumbled out into the command deck corridor. Peri straightened up when he saw Selene being led towards them under armed guard.

She tried to smile at them, but she seemed too nervous. Her eyes widened and she nodded towards a figure being led down the corridor in front of her.

It was Jaxx.

Peri felt his circuits shiver. General Pegg had summoned all four of them to the command deck. He must have reached a decision about their mission. And, if Selene and Jaxx were still under arrest, then that decision surely included punishment.

How much trouble are Diesel and I in? he wondered.

Again Peri touched the badge that General Pegg might be about to take away from him. He didn't regret anything he and his crew had done. They had saved the Milky Way! That had to count for something. He only hoped that the general hadn't found out that they had harboured a Meigwor bounty hunter on their ship. If Otto had been discovered, Peri knew that he and Diesel wouldn't just be dismissed from the IF – they'd be imprisoned.

They followed Jaxx and Selene into the packed Command Centre. The emperor was sitting with the royal family at one end, while IF Star Fighters and commanding officers filled the rest of the room. As soon as the door closed behind Peri, the room erupted into applause and cheers.

Some of the Star Fighters were cheering 'Peace in space!' while younger members of the royal family chanted Diesel's real name, Diaxo. Peri spotted his parents off to the side. They were both beaming at him.

Then he noticed that some of the crowd were also chanting for Selene and Jaxx. He felt a tingle of relief. *Surely no one would be cheering us if we're in trouble?*

General Pegg raised his hands and the room fell silent. 'Selene.' He beckoned to her.

Selene took a deep breath, straightened her tool belt and stepped forward.

'There is a long list of charges against you,' said the general, 'from breaking IF security protocol to stowing away on IF bases. In addition to this, we have found unauthorised changes to the *Phoenix* –'

'I was just fixing her!' Selene interrupted.

'Quiet,' the general replied. 'I should send you to space-detention. You clearly have no respect for authority, and find it impossible to obey orders.'

'Sir, if I might –' Peri started.

'No, Peri,' the general said. 'Nothing you

will say will change my mind. After reviewing the mission reports and all available data, it is my opinion that Selene is . . .' He paused and glanced at the serjeant-at-arms in his ceremonial uniform. 'An essential part of the *Phoenix*'s crew. Despite your lack of formal training, you are one of the brightest engineers we have ever seen, and so very brave too. Selene, please repeat after me.'

As Selene recited the IF creed, warm energy flowed through Peri's circuits. His engineer friend was now officially part of their crew! The general pulled a titanium badge from the box held by the serjeant-at-arms and pinned it to Selene.

'You are now a Star Fighter,' General Pegg declared.

There was a cheer of 'Peace in space' from the guests, before the general raised his hand for silence again.

Selene's smile vanished as he turned to Jaxx. Peri felt the warmth drain from his circuits as he realised that her father might still be punished.

The general took a deep breath. 'We're very sorry to have wrongfully accused you of being a space pirate. By order of His Imperial Majesty the Emperor, you are cleared of all charges. If you are happy to agree, we would like to appoint you as the IF's chief technician.'

Jaxx smiled and nodded. 'It would be an honour.'

'Sir,' Peri asked, 'what about Daxx and Tonka?'

'Daxx is in prison,' said the general, 'and will be for a long time. Unfortunately Tonka Mezzoka managed to escape. However, thanks to the *Phoenix*, the IF has confiscated the Mezzanator and captured most of the key leaders of the Mezzoka Clan. Tonka won't be as powerful without them as he once was.'

The general paused and frowned. 'You youngsters have achieved something remarkable. I sent you out on a very simple mission – to capture Jaxx. Not only did you accomplish this and return the Heart of Mars, but you also found the time to bring down the Mezzoka Clan, something we've been trying to do for years! Peri, Diesel . . . Selene, I know you probably want to take a well-earned rest after all your adventures. But I need my best young Star Fighters back on the job immediately. Your next mission is even more dangerous and important than the last one. There's no time to lose.'

Peri shared an excited look with Diesel and Selene. He couldn't wait to get back on the *Phoenix* and defend the Milky Way once more. Now that all three of them were officially Star Fighters, he felt ready to take on an entire galaxy.

He looked at the general. 'What's the mission?'

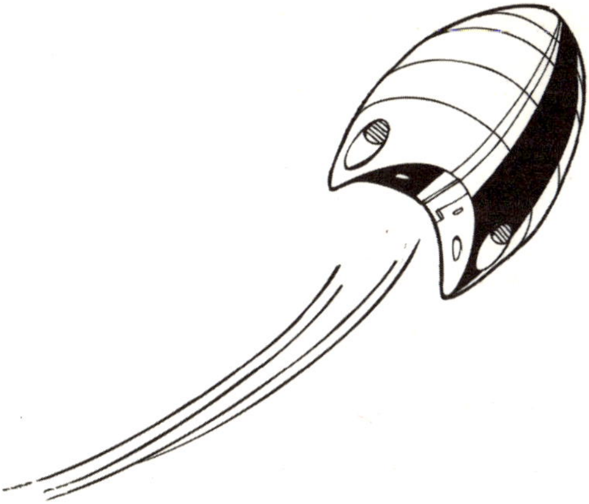

STAR FIGHTERS

Don't miss the next amazing

STAR FIGHTERS adventure!

Join Peri and the crew of the *Phoenix*
on their next mission!

Can they outwit a gang of outlaws
on a remote desert planet?

Find out! In . . .

STEALTH FORCE

COMING SOON!

Turn over to read Chapter 1

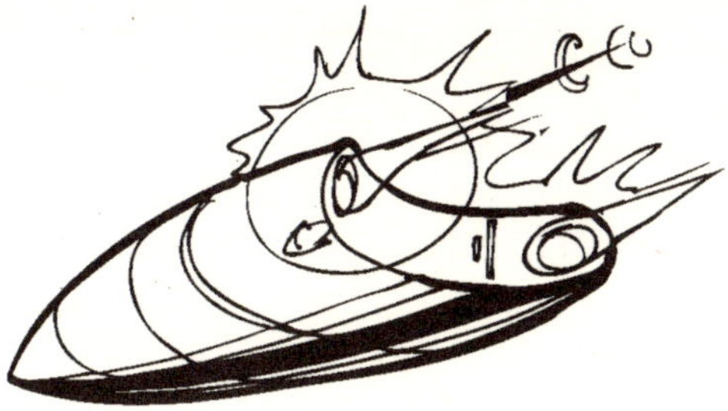

Chapter 1

'I'll tell you something interesting,' Anurack said, his four heads bobbing enthusiastically. He held up his fork. 'Something very similar to this green vegetable – which you call a "pea" – grows on Torganora, one of the planets of the Shantanian system in the Crab Nebula. But on that planet it's called a "blarp". That's very interesting, isn't it?' One of his heads looked at Peri, another at Diesel and another at Selene. The fourth just smiled at nothing in particular.

'Erm,' Peri said. 'That's *quite* interesting.'

'Yes, I knew you'd find it interesting,' Anurack said. He popped some chips into the mouth that had just spoken and began speaking from a different head. He was always switching his voice from one head to another. Keeping track of them made Peri dizzy. 'Now, you see this fork? On the planet Sklomp, they don't use forks – they use hollow wooden tubes to suck their food up. Of course, they eat porridge mainly. Isn't that just fascinating?'

Diesel rolled his eyes. Selene snorted, trying to suppress a giggle.

Peri shot her a warning look. It was very important not to offend Anurack: General Pegg had told them that Anurack's Galactic Federation were old allies of the Milky Way. The Star Fighters' assignment was simply to return him to his home planet of Koring, keeping him safe and happy. At cruising speed the trip took five days, but there were times when it had seemed more like five months to Peri. Anurack talked non-stop, and was surely the most boring sentient lifeform in the universe. And that was including the Talking Worms of Betelgeuse.

They had almost reached Koring and were having their last meal together in the *Phoenix* restaurant: a classic Earth-style feast of steaks, chips, peas and tomato ketchup, with fruit and ice cream to follow.

'This tomato ketchup,' Anurack said, as he dipped a chip, 'is red, which I believe is the colour of Earthlings' blood. On Jangananx they have a strange superstition where they can't eat anything the colour of their own blood, which is yellow. That means they can't eat bananas. What do you think of that?'

'I think it's really boring,' Diesel muttered.

Oh no! Peri thought. *Diesel's cracked – and we're so close to the end of this endless journey!*

General Pegg had promised that if the *Phoenix* crew carried out this mission on time and without incident, there would be another, much more exciting mission for them. But if they offended Anurack they'd probably all be grounded indefinitely.

All four of Anurack's heads swivelled in Diesel's direction. One of the heads looked puzzled, one looked suspicious and one looked hurt. The fourth looked all those things at once as it spoke. 'What did you –'

'Diesel said it was really, really *enthralling!*' Peri said, with a burst of inspiration.

Anurack's four heads smiled.

'That's it!' Diesel said. 'And very useful. If I ever go to Jangananx, I'll know not to go around offering everyone bananas!'

'Oh, but you could offer them bananas if they were peeled,' Anurack said. 'They love fruit on Jangananx. Do you know, it's been calculated that they eat 5,734 varieties of fruit there?'

Peri stole a look at his watch. They would be docking in fifty-three minutes. Fifty-three long minutes, each filled with sixty long seconds.

'Here we are!' Peri said, fifty-two minutes later. The grey-and-brown sphere of Koring filled the 360-monitor. 'Soon we'll be landing on Planet Boring – I mean, *Koring*.'

Selene snorted, just managing to contain her giggles. Diesel had gone and locked himself in his sleeping quarters on Peri's orders because they couldn't risk him upsetting Anurack.

'Koring's a very interesting planet,'

Anurack said. 'It orbits our sun at a mean average distance of 121 million kilometres. The atmosphere is composed of 17 different gases . . .'

Peri tuned Anurack out as he concentrated on easing off the boosters and adjusting the Nav-wheel to line the *Phoenix* up with the docking bay below. His special bionic connection with the ship made the tricky move feel simple and instinctive, as though he was manoeuvring his own body into position. A few moments later, the *Phoenix* came to rest neatly between the gates of the docking bay.

Peri breathed a sigh of relief. 'Welcome home, Anurack.'

He and Selene led Anurack off the Bridge and down a mauve-lit corridor. Peri sent a telepathic order to the *Phoenix* and watched the wall open noiselessly. A ramp extended itself down to the floor of the docking bay, where a group of four-headed Koringers were waiting.

'It's been a pleasant voyage,' Anurack said. 'I've enjoyed talking to you.'

Peri raised his voice to cover Selene's giggle. 'We enjoyed it too.'

'I'll let General Pegg know what a good job you did,' Anurack said. 'I only wish you could come and visit for a little while – I know everything there is to know about Koring, so I could give you a guided tour of the whole planet. You'd find it really interesting.'

'I'm sure we would, but we don't have the time,' Peri said.

He noticed a small timer had appeared in the bottom corner of the Mission Update screen on the control panel. It said, *120 hours, 0 minutes, 0 seconds and 0 tenths of a second.* As he watched, it began to count down, the tenths flickering away at lightning speed, the seconds ticking away steadily after them.

'Well, goodbye, then,' Anurack said.

Peri and Selene waved as Anurack walked down the ramp and the Koringers came forward to greet him.

'Welcome home, Anurack. Did you come back via the Horsehead Nebula?'

'No,' said Anurack, shaking all four of his heads. 'We used the Intergalactic Highway as far as Rigel, where we turned left on to the hyperspace bypass.'

'You should have gone via the Arcturan Wormhole,' another Koringer said, his heads frowning. There were so many heads now, Peri lost track of who was who. 'That's a quicker way. And there are more interesting things to see . . .'

Peri sent another telepathic order and the *Phoenix*'s wall closed, blocking the Koringers from view.

Selene punched the air. 'I'm glad that's over!'

Diesel emerged from hiding. 'Thank the Spirit of the Universe – Anurack's finally gone!' Diesel kicked his legs in the air for joy.

There was a light tap, and the *Phoenix*'s wall opened again silently. Anurack was standing at the end of the ramp.

Diesel, who had his back to the wall, carried on his high-kicking dance, chanting, 'He's gone, gone, *gone!*'

Two of Anurack's heads coughed. Diesel turned around and stopped laughing. His strip of hair turned pink with embarrassment.

There was an awkward silence.

'Erm, Diesel was just . . .' Peri faltered

for a moment, before his bionic circuits buzzed with an idea. 'Performing a traditional Martian farewell!'

'I'm acquainted with the customs of Mars,' one of Anurack's heads said, while the other three frowned. 'And I'm not aware of any such dance.'

'We do it all the time,' Diesel said. 'But only when the visitor has left . . . that's why you wouldn't have seen it.'

Three of Anurack's faces smiled. The fourth said, 'Ah, that explains it. An interesting fact to add to my collection! Well, I just forgot my hoverbag.' He beckoned, and the hoverbag rose up and floated along beside him as he exited once more.

Peri closed the wall. 'Let's get out of here before he comes back!'

Soon the *Phoenix* was cruising through outer space.

Peri spoke into the com-system. 'Bridge to Otto – the coast is now clear.'

A section of wall slid open and Otto came slouching on to the Bridge. He had had to hide while Anurack was on board because he was still technically a stowaway.

'Has he gone?' Otto said. 'It's been really boring cooped up in my quarters all this time.'

'Not as boring as being with Anurack!' Selene said.

'What's that?' Otto pointed with his long black tongue at the timer ticking down on the Mission Update screen. It now said, *119 hours and 47 minutes.*

'That's the countdown until our next mission,' Peri explained. 'We have to get back to the IF Space Station before it reaches zero or General Pegg will give our next mission to someone else.'

'Should we go Superluminal?' Diesel asked.

'No need, it's a waste of energy,' Peri said. 'We've got plenty of time, even if we travel at cruising speed.'

'We'd better!' Diesel said. 'I'm looking forward to another mission.'

'I hope I don't have to hide out on this one,' Otto grumbled. 'It's about time I got the chance to use my skills.'

'You haven't got any skills,' Diesel said.

'Oh, haven't I?' Otto boomed. 'Well, let me tell you, you Martian misfit . . .' He hissed and uncoiled one of his long arms, twirling it above his head.

Diesel squared up to him, jutting his chin out and clenching his fists.

'Ssshh!' Peri said, holding up his hand. 'What's that noise?'

Strange, low, rhythmic knocking sounds filled the Bridge.

Peri closed his eyes and tuned into the *Phoenix*'s computer. He felt an electric tingling as the noises gradually began to make sense. Peri had never learned Morse code, but the *Phoenix* knew it.

Dot dot dot dash dash dash dot dot dot . . .

'It's an SOS!' Peri said. 'Someone's calling for help!'

Have you checked out the **STAR FIGHTERS** website?
It's the place to go for games, downloads,
sneak previews and lots of cosmic fun! You can:

★ Blow up cosmic rubbish and shatter asteroids into a zillion pieces! Practise cosmic combat with the Star Blasters game!

★ Read all about your favourite cadets!

★ Download the Intergalactic Galaxy System Map!

★ Teleport your desktop to the IFA Space Station with out-of-this-world wallpapers!

★ Sign up for the Intergalactic Academy Force newsletter to get space-tastic extras and enter members-only competitions!

And there's much, much more so shuttle off to WWW.STARFIGHTERBOOKS.COM now!